P9-BZH-414

Jamie —

Maybe you'll read these to MACK — I really liked some of them —

God Bless —

Love, Baba + Granddaddy

5/9/99

PRAYERS FOR THE LITTLE ONES

ALSO BY JULIA CAMERON

The Artist's Way

The Money Drunk
(co-authored with Mark Bryan)

The Vein of Gold

*Heart Steps**

*Blessings**

The Artist's Way at Work
(co-authored with Mark Bryan and Catherine Allen)

The Right To Write

NOVEL
The Dark Room

POETRY
*This Earth**

*Prayers to the Nature Spirits**

*also an album with music by Tim Wheater

PRAYERS FOR THE LITTLE ONES

Julia Cameron

RENAISSANCE BOOKS

Los Angeles

Copyright © 1999 by Julia Cameron

All rights reserved. Reproduction without permission in writing from the publisher is prohibited, except for brief passages in connection with a review. For permission, write: Renaissance Books, 5858 Wilshire Boulevard, Suite 200, Los Angeles, California 90036.

Library of Congress Cataloging-in-Publication Data

Cameron, Julia.

    Prayers for the little ones / Julia Cameron.

       p. cm.

    Summary: A collection of forty-eight rhyming prayers arranged in three categories, prayers for young children, prayers for school children, and multi-faith religious prayers that address specific spiritual traditions.

    ISBN 1-58063-048-0 (alk. paper)

    1. Children—Prayer-books and devotions—English. [1. Prayers.] I. Title.

BL625.5.C35   1999

242'.82—dc21   98-51023

                                           CIP

                                           AC

10 9 8 7 6 5 4 3 2 1

Design by Lisa-Theresa Lenthall

Distributed by St. Martin's Press

Manufactured in the United States of America

First Edition

I dedicate this book to Timothy Wheater
Who asked me to write some prayers in meter.

CONTENTS

A   WORD   TO   PARENTS

While many adults remember and can recite the nursery rhymes of Mother Goose, very few of us remember many childhood prayers except:

Now I lay me down to sleep.
I pray the Lord my soul to keep.
If I die before I wake,
I pray the Lord my soul to take.

The key to our remembering this prayer is the fact that it is set in rhyme. It is like nursery rhyme, a small, simple poem that captures us both by its rhyme and its rhythm. So does another oft-remembered childhood prayer:

Angel of God, my guardian dear,
To whom God's love commits me here,
Ever this day be at my side,
To light, to love, to rule and guide.

In creating this book of children's prayers, I have chosen to work with rhyme. This allows the prayers to be easily memorized by both parent and child.

The book is divided into three separate areas: prayers for young children, prayers for school children, and ecumenical religious prayers for children from both age groups that address specific spiritual traditions. The third section allows children and parents to both focus on their own tradition and acquaint children with differing belief systems.

It is my hope that this book both reflects the spirit and feel of traditional children's spiritual works as well as the understandings that many modern parents have come to within their own spiritual practices.

PART ONE:
PRAYERS FOR YOUNG
CHILDREN

FRIENDSHIP PRAYER

God bless my friends at each day's start.

God hold them gently in your heart.

God bless my friends and keep them safe—

As they work and as they play.

God bless my friends at each day's end.

God gift them with sweet dreams. Amen.

SANTA PRAYER

This is a prayer direct to Santa Claus,

A letter to read before you take a pause.

I know I'm early and time's not here.

You only visit once a year.

Still, it helps to place my order

And gives you, Santa, a chance to barter.

You know what I'd like the best?

Give me that and all the rest!

FAMILY PRAYER

God bless my mom; God bless my dad.
God make them happy and not sad.
God bring our home your happiness.
God give us trust and gentleness.
Teach us, God, our time to spend
Loving our family as our friends.
Teach me, God, to do my part.
Give our home a loving heart.

ANGEL PRAYER

Angel walking by my side,
Keep me gentle as your tribe.
Let me see the good in souls—
The good in young ones and in old.
Show me how to see straight through
The hurtful things that people do.
Help me know good's still at hand
When life is hard to understand.

Bring me trust in gentle ways.
Guide me safely through my days.

ELDER PRAYER

Holy Elders gone to God,
Help me see my special job.
Show me through your higher view
The helpful things that I can do.
Although you're gone from earth below,
You're still watching me, I know.
I'm still listening for your voices.
I'd like guidance in my choices.
Use your age and greater sight
To guide me clearly to the right.
While we miss you here below,
We depend on guidance so,
Whisper, Elders, in my ear
And know that you are welcome near.

PRAYER TO SANTA'S ELVES

This is a prayer to Santa's Elves.
I know you've got the toys on shelves,
Stacked to the rafters and packed to
    the beams,
So why not pick me a thing that gleams?
I like the doll with golden curls,
And a satin dress and crown with pearls . . .

My brother goes for planes and trains.
You'd think a kid would have
    more brains.
My mother says, "to each his own."
Our dog is asking for a bone.
Our cat would like a lot of mice.
I don't think that is very nice.

Do your best, dear Santa's Elves,

To send us what we'd pick ourselves.

EASTER BUNNY PRAYER

This is a prayer to the Easter Bunny.

When you come hopping, I come running.

I love your chocolates and colored eggs

But really like your spring-like legs.

If I could jump the way you do

I'd be a human kangaroo.

I'd use my leaps to jump uphill,

Then tumble down to have a thrill.

I'd leap and bound through fields of flowers.

I could keep it up for hours.

Then I'd hop my way back home

And eat the chocolates you have borne.

INNER VOICE
PRAYER

God inside me, Little Voice,

Help me hear your gentle noise.

Help me listen as you talk.

Help me know the paths you walk.

Inner God who speaks in me,

Help me listen, help me see,

The gentle way, the loving trail.

Let me read you just like mail.

Spell for me with words and signs

The ways that are the best as mine.

Teach me, God, to go within

And always find you there, my friend.

HALLOWEEN PRAYER

This is a prayer to all Halloween Ghouls.

I hope you remember that this night

  has rules!

You're allowed to be scary—

But not very.

You're allowed to be seen,

But not to be mean.

I know enough to tell you, Goblins,

That exactly at midnight is when your

  job ends.

And so no nightmares as I sleep.

No scary thoughts to make me weep.

Instead, be like the jolly pumpkin,

Somewhat scary, more a bumpkin.

Keep your spooking like a joke.

Remember we are little folk!

GUIDANCE PRAYER

Guardian Guides, Helpful Tribe,

Always keep me by your side.

Higher Helpers, Higher Minds,

Let mine be a heart that finds

Divine Companions, Natural Friends.

Give me, please, a heart that tends

To look for beauty and for love,

A heart that like the gentle dove

Flies to heaven seeking good.

Guardian Guides, if you would,

Teach me, please, your graceful ways.

Guard and guide me through my days.

PART TWO:
PRAYERS FOR SCHOOL
CHILDREN

SIBLING PRAYER

This is a prayer to the God of Siblings.
Sometimes we fight but that's just quibbling.
Sometimes when I think of my brother,
I think I'd like to have another.
It's the same when you mention my sister,
But when she's gone I find I miss her.
We're really a family of friends, not of foes.
God, help me stop fighting my sisters
    and bro's!

BIRTHDAY PRAYER

This is a prayer to the God who made
  birthdays.
What a great plan—higher self-worth days!
No time like the present and the presents
  are mine,
That is, if I practice the presence of mind
To make all days special and not just the date
I elected to first participate.

Yes, I know that astrology's key,
But the use of the date is up to me.
And so I plan parties with cake and ice cream.
Sometimes I'm king and sometimes
  I'm queen.
Birthdays are equal in all they employ.
The rule's plain and simple—simply enjoy!

CAMPING PRAYER

This is a prayer to the Angel of Camping.

I'm tired of mosquitoes and slapping

and stamping.

My tent has a leak. It's a lake when it's rainy.

How'd I come camping if I'm so brainy?

The food all smells moldy.

My sandwich smells dead.

My trail mix is bird seed despite what

they said.

All of my power bars leave me quite weak.

They taste just like cardboard and stick

to my teeth.

I've got a terror of meeting a bear.

There's one right here somewhere. I just

don't know where.

continued

And as to what really gives me the shakes,

Have I mentioned my horror of spiders
   and snakes?

Angel of Camping, your job is cut out.

Be sure to come quickly if you hear a shout!

OUCH PRAYER

This is a prayer to the Angel of Ouch.

You know who I am. I am the grouch

With skinned shins and bruised bones and
  scratches from brambles.

It seems I get banged up on all of my rambles.

Angel of Ouch, I took a deep breath.

And I know that what hurts me is not
  sudden death.

Mercurochrome, iodine, pass the Bactine.

Couldn't you, Angel, invent a vaccine?

Something to keep me from biting my lip,

Something like Zorro to give trouble the slip?

I've counted to ten and kissed myself better.

Angel of Ouch, please count this a letter.

What I'm really after is your help before

continued

My finger encounters the slam of that door.

I guess what I'm saying is, "I want attention!"

Stop curing my woes and give me prevention!

TUMMY PRAYER

This is a prayer to the God who made
tummies.
Please tell my parents to give me more
yummies.
What's wrong with Gummy Bears, licorice,
and cake?
Why do they act like ice cream's a mistake?
They're down on soda pop. Ix-nay on candy.
It takes an act of God to score pecan sandie.
Don't mention brownies.
Forget chocolate chips.
I once had a Popsicle but that was a slip.
"You don't want a cavity," they always say.
World peace lacks gravity compared
to decay.

continued

Oh, God who made tummies,

    my sweet tooth's not loose.

Couldn't you tell them dessert's the caboose?

I'm sure you're following my train

    of thought.

Bribe me with sweets and I'll eat what

    I ought.

Pie, please, for breakfast. Pot pie for a snack.

Devil's food, angel food, peas after that.

Fudge before spinach! Kool-aid, then milk.

An end to the accidents of all that I've spilt.

God who made tummies, think appetizer.

A spoonful of sugar will make me much wiser.

FEVER PRAYER

Angel of Fevers, please give me a break.

Just how much suffering can a kid take?

I'm stuck in bed. I've still got a degree.

My parents are sounding like Simon Legree.

My friends are out playing. I'm laying around.

My Mom hears my cough, doesn't "like
    how it sounds."

Even the TV is starting to pale.

How would you feel with Walt Disney
    and jail?

Angel of Fevers, please do your tricks.

Thermometer, speedometer, 98.6!

MOVIE PRAYER

This is a prayer to the Angel of Movies.

Of all of God's Angels, you are the grooviest.

Thank you for giving us stories we watch.

I love all movies, even ones that you botch.

I love happy endings. I love finding gold.

Movies with villains are fun for the bold.

Gorillas, Godzillas, Giants with claws.

Movies obey their own set of laws.

Thank you for movies that glow in the dark.

Thank you for movies that give me the spark

To know I'm a hero with adventures ahead.

(Dreams are just movies that play in my bed.)

Thank you for heroines and special effects.

Thank you for movies the critics reject.

Movies are perfect despite all their failings.

Movies are good for whatever is ailing.

Just try a movie next time you're sad.

It will make you feel better even if it is bad.

Bad movies are good. Good movies are better.

Help me remember I should take a sweater.

Popcorn and sodas, the line forms to the right.

I could watch movies from morning to night.

Angel of Movies, don't tell me your plot.

I will watch gratefully whatever you've got.

MANNERS PRAYER

This is a prayer to the Angel of Manners.

I'm not really such a fan of yours.

Always say "thank you," my folks say—

Even for things that ruin my day.

Thanks for reminding me I need to study.

I'm sure that it really means you're

    my buddy.

Thanks for telling me to clean my room.

It only feels like impending doom.

"Please" is another word I'm told to try.

Please pass the peas and don't ask why.

Angel of Manners, if you ask me I'm

    doubtful

Why should I master such a bitter sweet

    mouthful?

Manners are better is all that I'm told—
I'll like manners better when I get old.

NEATNESS PRAYER

Angel of Neatness, I'm calling on you.

I know you're here somewhere—There!

In the shoe?

I know that you're tidy.

I know that you're neat.

I know you make parents especially sweet.

Angel of Order, please come to my room.

Be wary. It's scary as Dracula's tomb.

Toys all a jumble, clothes all a mess!

I know you've seen messes, but mine are

the best!

Crayons in the bedsheets, crumbs down

there, too,

Building blocks, filthy frocks, sandwiches—

goo.

Angel of Neatness, I must have your help.

My mother is simply beside of herself.

"Am I seeing double?" she wanted to know.

The mirror mirrored the mess so I said,

    "yes" and so

I'm grounded, you see, 'til I pick up my room.

Angel of Neatness, I've sealed my own doom.

Angel of Tidy, Angel of Clean,

I know that I've treated you awfully mean,

But if you'll appear and help tidy this mess,

Of all the Angels, I'll treat you the best.

STUDY PRAYER

This is a prayer to the Angel of Study.

School work is hard and I need a buddy.

History, Geography, English, and Math—

Sometimes they seem an impossible task!

It would help me a lot in learning my lessons

If you could teach me to see all the blessings

Of knowing my sums and where
    everything comes from,

Of learning my grammar with less of a
    stammer.

I know there's a point and a purpose to
    schools,

But sometimes it all seems like so many rules!

Angel of Study, I know you've excelled

So help me to do things a little more well.

Yes, I mean "better," that's just what's
the matter!

You hit home runs while I'm just a batter.

Angel of Study, please play ball with me.

A, I'll do better, and B, you will see.

You'll collar a scholar; you'll quiz
with a whiz!

You'll find I'm quite willing, the real
problem is

To do well at my schoolwork, I just need
a friend.

Angel of Study, that's where you come in.

PLAY PRAYER

I'm sending a prayer to the Angel of Play.

The one who knows safety and

    saving the day.

I'd welcome your guidance on having

    some fun—

Games that are smart, not games that

    are dumb.

Steer me from traffic that frantically roars.

Steer me away from all bullies and bores.

Find me some playmates gleeful like me.

Teach us to play games from A down to Z.

I like to play marbles and baseball and chess.

Tic-tac-toe, tag, and jacks also rate "yes"!

Indoors or outdoors, upstairs or down,

I can play anywhere that we can clown.

The world is my apple with fun at its core.

Angel of Play, pray, let me play more!

FRIENDS PRAYER

This is a prayer to the Angel of Friends,
The one who makes arguments
    instantly end.
The Angel of Kinship, the Angel of Pals,
The Angel of Best Friends who instantly solves
All disagreements and genuine fights
With the surprising surmising
    that both friends are right.

Angel of Buddies, Angel of Chums,
Please touch my friendships so each one
    becomes
Friendly and funny and loving and dear.
In other words, Angel, always stay near!

GOODNESS PRAYER

This is a prayer to the Angel of Good.
You know I'd be like you, I would if I could
Get over the notion that naughty is fun
Or warm to the motion of walk over run.
Angel of Good, tell the truth, is it true
Life can be fun when there's none to undo?
Come when I'm called, sleep when
      I'm told?
Angel of Good, I'll be young when I'm old!
Staying up late, never clearing my plate,
Breaking my toys—
      all of these have their joys!
Angel of Good, why not make me a deal?
You simply give me what I want to steal.
Help me with lies, help me with cheat!

continued

Help being sneaky's especially neat.

What's that, you say? Good's got more to
offer?

Pardon me, angel, but I'm a scoffer—

Bad feels good to me—

    that's why I'm praying.

If you are good, then you'll know what

    I'm saying.

Angel of Good, I am so good at bad,

If I change, a miracle is what we've had!

PARENT PRAYER

This is a prayer to the Angel of Folks,

The one who keeps playing such

    practical jokes

As giving nice parents to someone

    like me,

Who likes being naughty as naughty can be.

Angel of Dads, is it true as Dad tells

That he did the same things for which he

    now yells?

Did Dad break some windows?

Did Dad tease a cat?

Did Dad call his best friend something

    worse than a rat?

Angel of Folks, if these stories are true,

What is a youngster like me supposed to do?

continued

Did Mom pinch her sister, pull her hair,
    steal her money?
Is that why when I do these things she
    acts so funny?
Angel of Parents, apparently so!
Takes one to know one, the old saying goes.
And so, Guiding Angel of my funny folks,
Teach us to love us or give up the hoax.
Angel of Parents, guardian of mine,
Tell them that actually I'm doing fine.

ANGEL GUIDE
PRAYER

Angel Guide, God's friend to me,

Help me watch and learn to see

Every person is a saint.

It just takes time to contemplate

The good that's hiding in the bad,

The joy that's hiding in the sad.

Angel Guide, please give me sight

So I can know the wrong from right.

Guide me daily as I play,

As I study, as I pray.

Angel Guide, stay close to me.

Help me see what's meant to be.

FAMILIAR SAINTS PRAYER

This is a prayer to Saints I've known,

With whom I've shared an earthly home.

I know your name. You know my face.

I believe there is a place

For friendships lasting well past death.

You're with me still in every breath.

I call your name when I feel lost.

I know you hear me though you've crossed.

Gentle Saints, remember me.

I call on you for sympathy.

When I suffer, you send help.

Familiar Saints, I've always felt

You know me best, you love me true.

Please know that I remember you.

I know your goodness sure as gold,

And God must surely you enfold.

Familiar Saints, please, work with me.

Shape my higher destiny.

Familiar Saints, please guide my path.

I'll look forward as you look back.

Familiar Saints, please take my hand.

Guide my heart to understand

The longer view, the higher ground.

Familiar Saints, please stay around.

BICYCLE PRAYER

This is a prayer to the God of Bikes.

You've heard before from other tykes.

Bikes are fine, I have to say,

But tell me why they have to sway?

It's all balance, I am clear,

But could you help me past my fear?

Foot on the pedal, seat in the saddle,

I'd love to get on and simply skedaddle,

But I start to wobble when puddles arise.

Me and my bike hate a surprise.

Sudden gravel and I unravel.

A bike's a shaky way to travel.

You've heard before from kids like me,

Of battered hands and wounded knees.

God of Bikes, please teach me poise,

Just like the older girls and boys.

Teach me joy and teach me thrill,

But mostly teach me not to spill.

BUG PRAYER

This is a prayer to the God of Spiders

And all of the crawling inchers and gliders

Bugs are the best when seen from afar—

Although I like some of them well in a jar.

Bugs can be scary—and some of them furry.

I don't know where they go in such

    a hurry.

Bugs love to scurry and scoot out of sight.

Bugs in the kitchen all come out at night!

Cockroach and silverfish, centipede, ant—

Bugs can fit places the rest of us can't.

Bugs hide from big feet in cupboards and

    drawers.

Bugs know we'd rather keep bugs out

    of doors.

God of All Bugs, you who made them

    so scary.

Help me, like bugs, to be daring and merry.

God of All Bugs, bugs can bug me, that's all.

Please teach me to love them—after all,

    they're so small.

TEACHER PRAYER

This is a prayer to the God of Teachers—

How could you make such terrible

    creatures?

Teachers are scary! Teachers are strict!

Teachers make rules and make sure

    that they stick.

Teachers, when teaching, try hard to be nice

But nice is a word which seldom applies

To the frown which appears

When our grammar veers

Into the spheres that are met by "Oh dears."

"Oh dear," teacher says when I say, "I ain't."

("I ain't" among kids is a common complaint.)

I ain't done with homework.

I ain't good at math.

I ain't good at catching my "ain'ts"

    point of fact.

Teacher gets crabby. Teacher acts sad.

I get quite jumpy when teacher acts mad.

God of All Teachers, they won't go away.

So please give our teachers some small

    sense of play.

Teach them to smile, to say thank you

    and please.

Manners are nice in a teacher, you see.

Teach all our teachers to teach us with love.

If you can't manage that, then please make

    them eat grubs.

TOY PRAYER

This is a prayer to the God of Toys,
Whistles and bells and things that
    make noise.
Thank you for trucks and choo choo trains.
Thank you for cards and Monopoly games.
Thank you for jacks—thank you for Jills—
Thank you for things that give us such
    thrills
As dolls that can walk and wet and speak.
Now they speak English, soon they'll
    speak Greek!
Thank you for Teddy Bears.
Thank you for Beanies.
Thank you for Aladdins and lamps filled
    with Genies.

Thank you for Christmas and stockings
    you've stuffed
With so many toys they are almost enough.
Thank you, above all, for knowing our greed
For more toys to explore, toys beyond
    any need.
Thank you for giving us toys by the score.
And thank you for knowing we will
    always want more!

NUMBERS PRAYER

God of Math, God of Numbers,

I need your help when I make blunders.

You invented one plus two.

And you know why numbers multiply, too.

As for me, I feel divided,

Half loves Math and half's decided

That numbers add up to lots of trouble—

Which means this prayer asks you to double

The brains I have for doing sums.

Please make me smart instead of dumb.

Please teach me add and then subtract.

Please help me learn to love my math.

Two plus two? The answer's four.

But I need help in keeping score.

When we get as far as fractions,

I am prone to grave distractions.

Dewey decimals do me in.

This is why I need a friend.

Oh, God of Numbers, hear my cry

And help me learn to work with pi.

Abracadabra! Give me the magic

To find my Algebra less than tragic.

Teach me Geometry—triangles, squares,

By answering, God, my mathematical prayers!

TOOTH FAIRY
PRAYER

This is a prayer to the Tooth Fairy.

Losing a tooth is very scary.

It all begins with a little wobble

Which makes our food quite hard to gobble.

Next, the tooth begins to sway.

It moves a little more each day.

Soon it's barely in your head—

And here's the part I really dread.

My mother says, "Just let me pull it."

But I cannot bite the bullet.

She hopes, I guess, that I'll say "Yes"

And volunteer for my distress.

"It won't hurt" is what she tells me.

I can't believe such lies are healthy.

Finally she sits me in a chair—

And says, "Why see, it's barely there!"

Then she gives a sudden tug

And hands me hankies if there's blood.

It's quite an awful situation

And so you enter the equation.

Late that night as I lie sleeping—

After I am done with weeping—

You, Tooth Fairy, come to visit

With money for my pain exquisite.

Please, Tooth Fairy, grant my wish

And find a way your job to switch.

Let my teeth fall out more freely,

That way I can love you really.

READING PRAYER

This is a prayer to the Angel of Reading

Who knows precisely the help I'll be needing

With words like "through"

Pronounced like "do"

And words like "tough"

That are said like "rough."

That's just a few but it's enough

To start a reader really spinning.

Dick and Jane are the beginning.

Then "ball" and "bat" and "throw"
    and "strike"

As Dick and Jane meet Pat and Mike.

Reading teems with teams, you see—

And rules to sort out the debris

Like "i" before "e" except after "c."

Reading is not a democracy.

Reading rewards all the trouble it takes

By spelling delicious words, candies

    and cakes.

Sugar and chocolate, jelly and jam,

"Ice cream" will show you the reader I am.

I scream for simple words all in a row.

Angel of Reading, please help me to know.

Which sounds are silent and which sounds

    are heard.

Let me read "sing song" like I'm a bird.

PART THREE:
ECUMENICAL PRAYERS

CREATOR PRAYER

Creator God, who made the earth,

Teach me what our planet's worth.

Give me love for every tree,

For every bird, for every bee.

Give me love for hills and valleys,

For city streets and city alleys.

Give me love for foreign lands,

And give me love that understands.

Our earth is whole and we are holy.

Our earth is one and we are only

Loving friends who haven't met.

The best is yet to come, I'll bet.

MOTHER EARTH
PRAYER

Mother Goddess, cloaked in green,

Help us know your gentle dream.

Wreathed in willow, sheathed in corn,

Bathed in moon and swathed in sun,

Green Gold Goddess, Mother Earth,

Help your children know their worth.

Herb and flower, ant and granite,

All are brethren on this planet.

Teach us, Mother, how to see

The wisdom of equality.

Grace our minds with the knowledge

All around us is a college.

We can learn from running brook

As surely as from any book.

Aspen, Pine, Balsam, Fir,

All of these our teachers are—

Lark and Eagle, Squirrel and Sparrow,

Teach us to be broad not narrow.

Goddess Green, our finest teacher,

Give us grace to know our nature.

GRANDMOTHER MOON PRAYER

This is a prayer to Grandmother Moon,
Whose silver light can paint my room,
Whose shiny face can light the night
And teach me to know wrong from right.
Grandmother Moon, you change faces.
Let me learn to know the places
Where I should hide and I can shine,
Whom to avoid, who're friends of mine.
Teach me, Elder, your discretion.
Place me under your protection.
As you've learned to wax and wane,
Teach me how to use my brain.

FATHER SKY PRAYER

This is a prayer to Father Sky,

Taller than trees, much taller than I.

Father Sky, so cool and blue,

Help me to take the higher view.

Help me know on days of rain,

The sun will always shine again.

Teach me, too, when nights are dark

That dawn will always bring the spark

Of sunny skies and snowy cloud.

Teach me, Father, I'm allowed

To change my mood as you do yours.

Yet teach me, Father, what endures.

It's love that's large and high and tall,

Says Father Sky who loves us all.

CHRIST PRAYER

Christ Child, Jesus, gentle friend,
The King of old Jerusalem,
Teach me how to sweetly pray,
To love my friends and sweetly play.
Teach me, please, for all I meet.
Help me be both true and sweet.
Christ Child, Jesus, gentle friend,
Like you, help me your flock to tend.
Sweetly shepherd, gently guide,
Me and others to your side.
Baby Jesus, bless me here.
Keep me safe and keep me near.

MARY PRAYER

Mary Mother, dressed in blue,

Guide and guard me all day through.

Teach me what you taught to Christ—

To love my friends and treat them nice.

Mary Mother, Queen of Saints,

As you watch from heaven's gates,

Bless this child of yours below.

Like a flower, help me grow.

JOSEPH PRAYER

Father Joseph, Jesus' Dad,

Teach me like you taught the lad.

Teach me, Joseph, gentle skills

That Jesus learned in Israel's hills.

Teach me kindness; teach me faith.

Teach me, Joseph, to obey

The lessons learned through carpentry—

To polish the wood in what I would be—

I would be gentle. I would be kind.

I would be friendly and I would try

To walk like you do in gentle strength.

Father Joseph, be my friend.

DAVID PRAYER

David, singer of the Psalms,

Make my heart a loving balm.

Help me live the gentle notes

Your heart heard and gently wrote.

David, teach me sing God's praise.

Praise the nights and praise the days.

Praise the moon and praise the sun.

See God's face in every one.

David, poet for our tribe,

Like you, let me be a scribe,

Writing glory be to God!

David, thank you for your job.

KRISHNA PRAYER

Dear Lord Krishna, Flute of God,

Call me gently to your side.

Let me hear the tunes you bear

That teach us love and teach us care.

Dear Lord Krishna, pipe for me.

Help me join life's symphony.

Teach me sing in unison

With all the friends your blessings

    bring.

Lord of Music, Lord of Song,

Help me to know right from wrong.

Teach me life in harmony.

Embracing love as shore the sea.

Lord of Pipers, Lord of Dance,

Help me to take every chance

To fill this world with melody,

To love my friends but set them free.

MOHAMMED PRAYER

Lord Mohammed, prophet wise,

Guide my heart to know its size.

Teach me to see God in all

To know that each is wonderful.

Lord Mohammed, desert soul,

Teach me to embrace the whole.

Help me see the truth of life,

The beauty holding even

    in strife.

Lord Mohammed, prophet wise,

Teach my heart to gently prize

My fellow travelers as my friends,

My journey for the gifts it brings.

Lord of Wind and Lord of Sand,

Teach my heart to understand

All is one when clearly seen.

Teach me, Prophet, what you mean.

BABA PRAYER

Baba gentle, Baba dear,

Baba, call your children near.

Teach us love and teach us serve.

Teach us by the gentle curve

Of loving smile and loving word

To know the truth of brotherhood.

Baba, Father, Friend to all,

Loving equal, large and small.

Hand of kindness, heart of love,

Make me, Baba, like the Dove,

Sweet in nature, sweet in sound,

Gentle, Baba, to be around.

Baba gentle, Baba dear,

Teach my heart to lose its fear.

Show me, Baba, how to see

The Golden Age of unity.

Baba gentle, Baba dear,

Thank you for your presence here.

GURU PRAYER

Gentle Guru, clothed in flame,

Softly let me speak your name.

Sacred Teacher, Heaven's Help,

Show me how to love myself.

Holy One who leads me here,

Help me find and disappear

Into oneness, into love.

Help me go within because

Loving God inside of me,

I find the God in all, you see.

Sacred Teacher, Sacred Friend,

Bless my heart and help it mend.

Earthly troubles, earthly woes.

Let mine be a faith that grows.

BUDDHA PRAYER

This is a prayer to Baby Buddha,

The one who knows me even better

Than I sometimes know myself.

Buddha teaches inner wealth.

Buddha teaches me stop trying.

Buddha teaches me stop crying.

All you need is yours already.

Buddha, teach me to be steady,

Even-tempered, loving, calm.

Buddha teaches me the song

Of loving one through loving all.

Buddha knows no large or small.

Buddha holds all beautifully.

Buddha teaches, so do we.

HEAVENLY HOST PRAYER

Host of Angels, Higher Friends,

Show me how our nature blends.

Teach me listen to Higher Me.

Teach me climb to where I'm free.

Life gets fearful here below.

I go too fast. I go too slow.

Angel Teachers, set my stride.

Walk beside me at my side.

Slow me down if there is need.

Take my hand to give me speed.

Host of Angels, Higher Friends,

Teach me that creation tends

To flow with purpose and with grace.

Angel Teachers, set my pace.

ABOUT THE AUTHOR

Julia Cameron, best-selling author of *The Artist's Way*, *The Vein of Gold*, *The Right To Write*, *Blessings*, *Heart Steps*, and *The Dark Room*, is an active artist who teaches internationally. A poet, playwright, novelist, essayist, and award-winning journalist, she has extensive credits in film, television, and theater. Cameron's poetry album, *This Earth* (music by Tim Wheater), won *Publishers Weekly's* Best Original Score award.